#4

MARVEL

A BLACK PANTHER ADVENTURE

SHURI

WAKANDA FOREVER

WILKERSON 19

SHURI

BY NIC STONE

SCHOLASTIC INC.

ABDOBOOKS.COM

Reinforced library bound edition published in 2021 by Spotlight, a division of ABDO, PO Box 398166, Minneapolis, Minnesota 55439. Spotlight produces high-quality reinforced library bound editions for schools and libraries. Reprinted by permission of Scholastic Inc.

Printed in the United States of America, North Mankato, Minnesota.
092020
012021

First printing 2020

Book design by Katie Fitch

Library of Congress Control Number: 2020942439

Publisher's Cataloging-in-Publication Data

Names: Stone, Nic, author.
Title: Wakanda forever / by Nic Stone
Description: Minneapolis, Minnesota : Spotlight, 2021. | Series: Shuri: a Black Panther adventure; #4
Summary: Shuri and K'Marah rush back to Wakanda in order to attend Challenge Day, but a mysterious enemy blocks them from the palace and threatens to destroy the dwindling heart-shaped herbs.
Identifiers: ISBN 9781532147760 (lib. bdg.)
Subjects: LCSH: Shuri (Fictitious character)--Juvenile fiction. | Wakanda (Africa : Imaginary place)--Juvenile fiction. | Princesses--Juvenile fiction. | Adversaries--Juvenile fiction. | Adventure and adventurers--Juvenile fiction. | Black Panther (Fictitious character)--Juvenile fiction | Graphic novels--Juvenile fiction
Classification: DDC [Fic]--dc23

Spotlight

A Division of ABDO
abdobooks.com

FOR KALANI JOY AND ALL THE LITTLE BROWN-SKINNED SUPER-GENIUSES. STEAM ON, LOVES.

—NIC

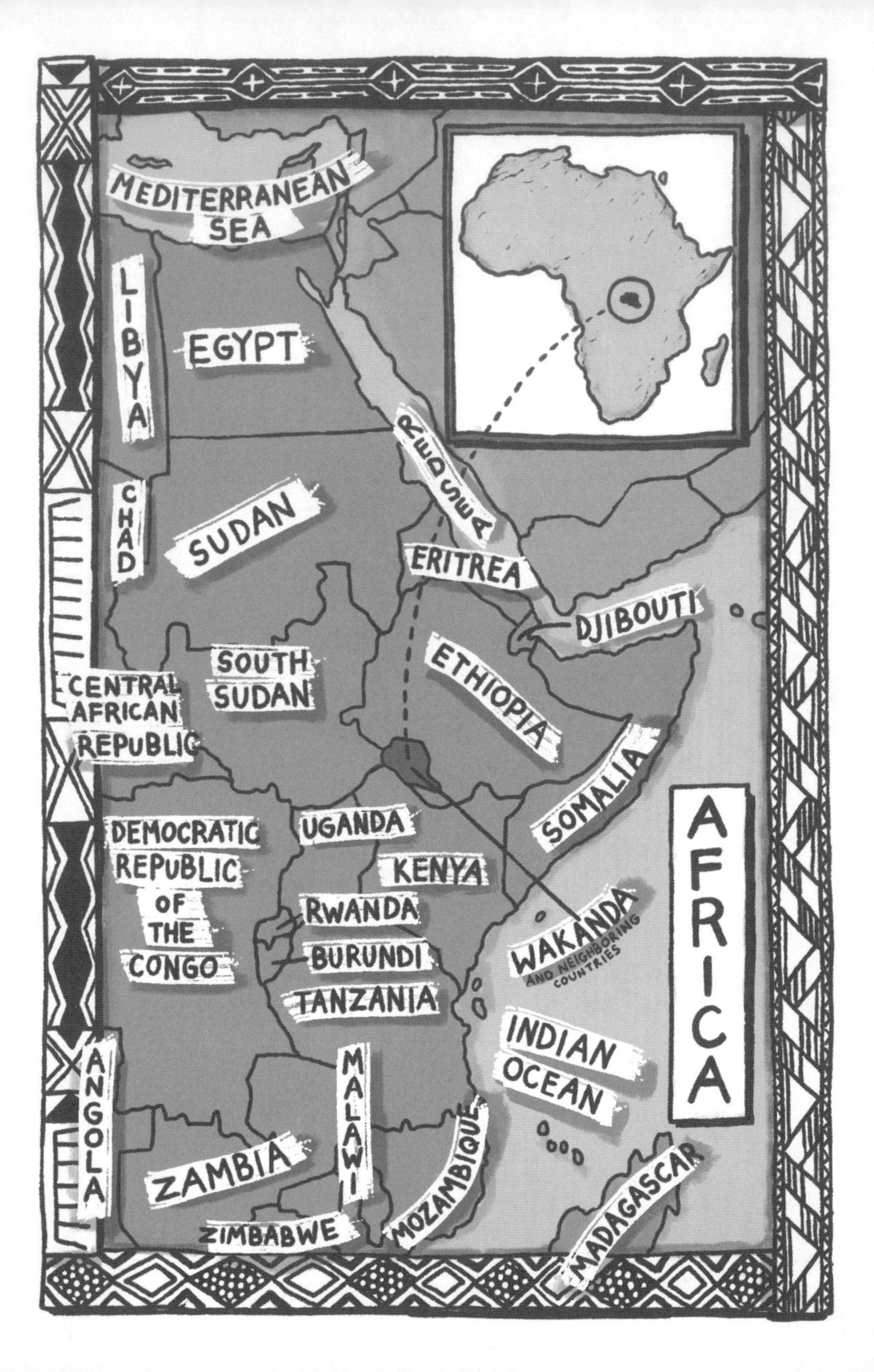
MEDITERRANEAN SEA
LIBYA
EGYPT
RED SEA
CHAD
SUDAN
ERITREA
DJIBOUTI
SOUTH SUDAN
ETHIOPIA
CENTRAL AFRICAN REPUBLIC
SOMALIA
AFRICA
DEMOCRATIC REPUBLIC OF THE CONGO
UGANDA
KENYA
RWANDA
BURUNDI
WAKANDA
AND NEIGHBORING COUNTRIES
TANZANIA
INDIAN OCEAN
ANGOLA
MALAWI
ZAMBIA
MOZAMBIQUE
MADAGASCAR
ZIMBABWE

WAKANDA
THE JABARI-LANDS
MOHANNDA
BIRNIN T'CHAKA
BIRNIN DJATA
BIRNIN BASHENGA
BIRNIN ZANA
(THE GOLDEN CITY)
NECROPOLIS
(THE CITY OF THE DEAD)
NYANZA
MENA NGAI
(THE GREAT MOUND)
CANAAN
BIRNIN S'YAN
BIRNIN AZZARIA
ALKAMA FIELDS
NIGANDA
AZANIA
N
W
E
S

18

SIGNS AND WONDERS

Shuri blinks.

Rubs her eyes . . . and blinks again.

"K'Marah?" she says to her friend. The girls are standing inside the *Predator*, which is still parked out behind the Den, staring at rotating holograms of identical molecules. "Are you seeing what I'm seeing?"

"If you mean matching ball-stick diagram thingies, then yes," K'Marah replies.

"It's a molecule. A pair of identical ones, in fact."

"I believe you, Princess."

And though the words floating *beneath* the matching molecules are *SUBSTANCE UNKNOWN*, the one above says *MATCH*.

And it's the only one that matters.

"K'Marah, *that* molecule," Shuri says, and points to the one on the right, "came from the bracelet you were wearing."

"You mean the one that was more or less sapping my life force?" Her eyes go stormy. "Just *wait* till I use some of your gadgets to pinpoint that idiot boy's home addr—"

"Yes. That bracelet," Shuri says. She takes a deep breath. "What's interesting is that the *other* molecule"—now she points to the one on the left—"was pulled from the roots of a dead heart-shaped herb plant."

"Huh." K'Marah rubs her chin.

"Right."

Shuri sees K'Marah's head cock to one side in her peripheral vision. "So . . . does that mean what I think it means?"

"What do you think it means?"

"That whoever made my—I mean *the*—bracelet is the reason your plants are dying?"

Shuri's eyes narrow. "Likely."

K'Marah snorts. "Figures."

"Huh? What figures?"

"That the first boy I really like would try to murder me."

They stand in silence for a few seconds longer, watching the matching molecules turn.

"So would I be right in assuming Henny—*if* that's even his name—has been working for that lanky loser we fought in London?"

"It's possible," Shuri replies. "Or lanky loser could be working for Henny. If that's his name." She pauses. "If it's a him, even."

"You think it's a girl?"

Shuri shrugs as the horrific face of the dry woman floats across her mind. "Could be either. Or neither. Or both. Not ruling anyone out."

K'Marah nods. "I hear that."

"The person is here," Shuri says, flicking her eyes to the GPS screen on the left. There's a blinking red dot at the base of the mountain region.

"Huh?"

"In Wakanda. I flipped the signal-tracing mechanism in your bracelet so that the tracker inside works *as* a tracker. When we were in the Den, I got a message that a signal was acquired—which means someone made an attempt to figure out where we are."

"Whoa."

"I'll admit, I wasn't expecting anyone to try to track us again. I figured with our London assailant incapacitated by our Wakandan cohorts, that would be that," Shuri says. "Tweaking the tech was more a . . . cautionary measure. In case we got lucky."

"Are you saying *this* is luck?"

Shuri shrugs again. "At least we have a lead."

"Okay . . . so whoever is looking for us is in the mountains now?"

The princess stares at the blinking dot. "Well, they *were*. The signal was lost."

"Do they know where *we* are?"

"Don't think so," Shuri says. "If I did my job right, they should've gotten an error message instead of a location for us."

"You clever little panther cub."

Shuri smiles. "Thank you."

"So, what now?"

The princess taps her bracelet, and the images disappear. "Have a seat and buckle up," she says, settling into her captain's chair and powering up.

K'Marah complies. "Where are we going?"

"To my lab," Shuri says. "I'll run some more tests and start the Vibranium infusion for T'Challa's new suit."

"Okay."

They rise in hover mode, and then take off.

"Umm, Shuri?"

"Yes, K'Marah?" Shuri wouldn't say it aloud right now, but her chest tightens at the sight of the capital disappearing beneath them. What if the invasion plans succeed?

"Not to be annoying, but then what?"

"Huh?"

"After you do the testing and suit thing?"

"Oh." It is an excellent question. "Well, then we wait."

"For?"

"For your bracelet-gifter to try to track us again."

"A-ha." K'Marah's eyes drop to her hands in her lap. "You really think they will?"

"Absolutely," Shuri says, steel in her voice now. "And when they do? We will find them."

The box of polyelastane fabric is waiting in the cavern hallway outside Shuri's lab door when the girls arrive. And to the princess's delighted surprise, it takes way less time than she anticipates to complete the infusion (such is the beauty of having a massive stash of refined Vibranium lying around). As soon as it's complete, she sends it by drone to the waiting clothier.

Shuri then starts a series of *new* tests on the substance from the bracelet and herb roots—to see its effects on variously sized machines. It turns out there are only trace amounts on the piece of jewelry, so whoever gave it to K'Marah didn't want *her* to die. But Shuri's hunch is that the same unknown substance used to kill the heart-shaped herb is also being used to create the entry path through the security forest for the invading army.

After the mechanical deaths of a spare Kimoyo card, a drone, and a four-wheeler Shuri sometimes used to travel between the palace and the lab—all made with or enhanced by Vibranium—she's fairly certain her hypothesis is correct. Interestingly enough, the substance has no effect on electronics *without* Vibranium, though it does utterly trash any organic matter it touches, including a mango, a black segmented millipede (Bast rest its many-legged soul), and a succulent plant Okoye brought to the princess from some place called California.

And then it happens.

The princess is tinkering with the "CatEyez" (the *z* was K'Marah's idea) just for the sake of killing time when her Kimoyo card buzzes like an angry wasp. "Ahh!" she jumps, not only dropping the tiny screwdriver she was using, but also bumping the edge of the lab table so hard, her entire tool kit goes crashing to the floor.

"Typical," K'Marah says from behind her.

"You know what—"

"Signal acquired," the computerized voice says with zero enthusiasm.

The girls look at each other . . . and both lunge toward the device.

"What's it say?" K'Marah asks, peeking over Shuri's shoulder.

Shuri stares at the red dot, now solid instead of flashing because the tracker is actively in use.

A spark of fury ignites inside her as the dot moves. "I should've known."

"What? Where is he? She—" K'Marah blows out a frustrated breath. "Where are they?"

"Close by. And moving through a different part of the forest," Shuri replies.

She looks at K'Marah. "They're headed to the Sacred Field."

19

HENBANE

After tucking two pairs of CatEyez into her knapsack, and grabbing a few of the "gentler weapon" prototypes—ones that disarm and disable, but don't destroy—from her arsenal, the princess and her mini Dora Milaje get on their way. It's a short journey to the field, and the little tracker-tracking light on Shuri's Kimoyo card screen stays solid through the duration of their trek.

Whoever is behind the bracelet, at least, is *definitely* in the field.

It's clear something is wrong as the girls stealthily

approach the concealed entrance: There's no one manning it.

Typically, Kufihli or one of the other priests would be standing guard on the other side to prevent intruders—wild animals, wandering children, or wannabe Black Panthers—from waltzing in.

But that's precisely what Shuri and K'Marah do.

It's dead quiet—no pun intended—and dark inside the cave-like space due to the lack of the herb's soft phosphorescence. Shuri didn't realize *how* incandescent the plants naturally are until just now. The lack of light is disorienting, especially since they can't utilize any other sources of illumination without giving themselves away.

But then she remembers—

"K'Marah," she whispers, "there are two pairs of those glasses I showed you down in the bag. Put one on and give me the other."

K'Marah does just that. "I . . . still can't see anything."

"Tap the right side and say 'scotopic-mode.'"

K'Marah complies, but as Shuri does the same and the area around them goes purple and bright through the lenses, she can see K'Marah shaking her head. "Of course she couldn't just call it *night vision*," K'Marah grumbles.

But then the shorter girl turns her head and—

"Shuri!" she whispers furiously, pointing to something in front of them and to the right. "Look!"

As Shuri's eyes slowly adjust, she can see a series of large lumps come into focus.

"Are they . . . dead, do you think?" K'Marah asks.

And that's when it crystallizes: The haphazardly distributed shapes are the collapsed—and hopefully just *unconscious*—forms of Kufihli and three of the priestesses.

"*Shuri!*" K'Marah hisses, more urgently this time.

"*Wha—*"

But Shuri sees *exactly* what. Back in the far-left corner of the field, some hundred meters or so away, a narrow swath of plants still faintly pulses with delicate light—and life.

Except right before Shuri and K'Marah's eyes, row by row, the lights dim and go out.

A bright blur passes over a pocket of the remaining glowing herbs, obscuring them from view for the breadth of a second. The princess gasps and risks a peek at her Kimoyo card. "K'Marah, he's over there! Come on!"

They advance, carefully, quietly, the silence of their movement assisted by the sound-absorbing, Vibranium-soled shoes both girls are wearing. When Shuri tossed

K'Marah her auto-contouring pair, the to-be Dora looked at the toed slippers and said, "What are these, *feet gloves*?"

Now she's changed her tune. "These toe huggers are *amazing*, Shuri!" she says. "I can't hear a thing!"

"Shhh!"

As they get closer, the rows of light begin to fade more quickly.

"We won't make it in time," Shuri says, stopping their progress. "Here, give me the gauntlet. This should knock him unconscious, but if I need the other thing, you remember the code word, right?"

"Yep." K'Marah unslings the bag again, and the princess reaches in to pull out a boxing glove-style mechanized hand-covering that's shaped like a panther's paw. She shoves her fist inside.

"Here goes . . ." Shuri says.

And she lifts her arm, aims, and squeezes the trigger.

A shoot of brilliant light bursts forth, illuminating the entire field as it zips over the sea of shriveled herbs.

But then halfway across, the light hits something and, if Shuri's not mistaken, gets absorbed. She watches rapt as the light spreads from the center of the object out to its edges—the thing is shaped like a sun. But then the motion reverses: The light returns from each pointed tip to recondense in the center . . .

And the princess has fiddled with enough Vibranium-based tech to know exactly what that means.

"DUCK!" she shouts at K'Marah, grabbing hold of her friend's arm and yanking her to the ground just as the ray of electroluminescent kinetic energy comes back at them from the core of the sun-shaped shield.

"Oh my gods!" K'Marah exclaims. "What was *that*?"

"I'm not entirely sure, but whoever is wielding it certainly knows their way around our most valuable resource. That shield is made of Vibranium!"

"But how—"

"Princess Shuri, I am most surprised!" comes a familiar female voice that makes Shuri feel as though her very blood cells are quivering apart within her veins.

"No . . ." she whispers under her breath. Her hands go damp, and despite the glasses, her vision begins to cloud at the edges.

"Shuri?" K'Marah grabs her arm, snatching her back into the present. "Who *is* that? Why does she know your name?"

"Firing on an opponent whose back is turned? How very dishonorable! I expected better from you," the woman says.

Bright light suddenly fills the space from somewhere above Shuri's head. "Who are you, and what do you want?" K'Marah's voice booms. She's now standing, CatEyez removed, with her Kimoyo card held aloft, flashlight cranked up to full power.

The woman just smiles.

And even without the jagged teeth, red eyes, and scarily cracked skin, her visage is terrifying.

The woman from Shuri's worst nightmares is . . . larger than the princess would've expected. Taller than T'Challa, and with broader shoulders, her hair braided in thick cornrows, she's wearing an ornately embroidered stomach-baring top and billowing black trousers that taper at the ankles beneath a long, sheer kimono-style robe. The image of Wakanda being crushed in her (rather large) hand floats to the surface of Shuri's consciousness.

She's behind all this.

Shuri taps the left side of the glasses this time. A see-through blue screen appears before her eyes with the words *Search Mode* across the top. "I need to find out who that woman is and where she came from," the princess whispers.

The head of a panther spins in front of her eyes as the info-search begins, but then—

SPECTACLES OFFLINE. NO SIGNAL DETECTED.

"Well, that's just wonderf—"

"Henbane!" the woman shouts over her shoulder at the plant killer.

Shuri taps to return to night-vision mode (how primitive, that phrasing) and returns her focus to the woman.

"Come!" she continues to her crony. "There is someone I'd like for you to meet." Another smile.

As the person approaches—indeed, a boy who's long-limbed and deep brown-skinned, a hair taller than Shuri, and maybe a year older—the princess glances past him to the back corner of the field. The fading has slowed, but after a quick scan and mental calculation, Shuri is certain that within twelve to fifteen minutes, the last of the heart-shaped herb plants will succumb to whatever plague this *Henbane* has wrought upon them.

"Henny?" K'Marah says from beside her. The boy looks up and locks eyes with Shuri's friend. The princess turns to look at her as well—and instantly looks away. She's never seen K'Marah so angry. And hurt. "Or *Henbane*, I guess, is your real name? Why would you do this?"

Shuri's not sure whether her friend is talking about his active murder of the heart-shaped herb or his betrayal of *her*. But either way, she also wants to know.

"Ah, don't blame him," the woman says. "He was merely completing the job I hired him for. He was an aimless street urchin when I found him, but after all this is finished and I accomplish *my* mission, he'll be one of the richest and most powerful young men in the Horn of Africa."

The boy drops his head.

"For too long," the woman continues, "Wakanda has stood idly by, cloaked from view, while the rest of the region suffers from drought and rising temperatures. Our water has dried up. Our crops are failing. Our people are *dying* from heat exhaustion and dehydration—"

"Wait a minute! I know who you are!" K'Marah says. "You were at the Pan-African Congress on the Treatment of Superhumans!"

Shuri tries to ignore the surge of jealousy over this *second* Very Cool Congress Thing K'Marah has attended. (What even is the *point* of being a "princess"?)

"You're Princess Zanda of Narobia!" K'Marah goes on. "*You* were in support of that wretched Superhuman Registration Act from America!"

Princess Zanda continues to smile, but Shuri can tell it's forced now. "As Henbane here will tell you, we are very good to the *mutants* that live among us in Narobia."

(Shuri doesn't miss the extra emphasis on the *m*-word.)

"None of *this* would've been possible without him, in fact! Isn't that right, Henbane?"

The boy doesn't say a word.

"This gifted young man was discovered in the act of draining the life from a pawpaw tree behind the home of a Narobian diplomat. He was frail. Dry-skinned and brittle-boned. A beggar orphan en route to becoming a common criminal—or worse." She turns to Henny, whose narrow shoulders rise and fall with a sigh, though he still hasn't lifted his head. "In him, I saw great purpose. A sense of *destiny*. So I took him under my wing and we formed a grand plan that would shove this haughty and uncharitable nation from its self-erected pedestal."

Shuri flinches but doesn't respond.

Zanda goes on. "Knowing of the soft spot your countrymen seem to have for orphaned children—including children descended from pale-skinned monsters who would seek to keep our entire *continent* subjugated—Henbane entered this nation through the mountain region some time back, and was swiftly taken in by your Jabari."

Now Shuri is so baffled, she *has* to speak. *"Really?"*

"Told you they weren't so bad," K'Marah says from beside her. "Though *he* clearly is."

And then *he* speaks. "K'Marah, I'm—"

"Silence, Henbane," Zanda commands.

"But I need to tell her tha—"

"You need to tell her—them—nothing but 'Goodbye.'" She shifts her focus back to Shuri and K'Marah. "Your precious herb is *gone*, so once we eliminate that arrogant brother of yours, there will be no *Black Panther* strutting around with an unfair advantage. While your beloved king is engaged in that sham of a 'ritual Challenge'—as if any *normal* person could best a superhuman—the joined armies of we neighboring countries you neglect will invade this selfish nation. Troops have already begun their journey through a path our beloved Henbane set into motion through your border forest this morning."

Shuri shakes her head then. "They'll be stopped as soon as they cross the border. T'Challa already knows—"

"T'Challa knows NOTHING!" Zanda spits.

"Someone's delusional," K'Marah murmurs.

But Zanda rails on: "When I have secured access to your Vibranium and control over your goods and technology, I will be able to *assist* those who are suffering and dying in neighboring nations, as well as sell off some of your precious resources to interested buyers. I will appear to the wider world as wise, rich, *and* benevolent. And Narobia will finally receive the place of prominence it deserves on the international stage," she says, lifting her arms and sun shield into the air.

"Delusional," K'Marah says again.

Shuri risks a flick of her eyes past Zanda and sees that there are two rows of herbs left. Maybe ten plants total. She wishes she could focus there longer so she could estimate the rate at which they're fading into uselessness.

"Hey, S.H.U.R.I! What time is it?" Shuri shouts.

"The time is four thirty-seven p.m.," the voice replies from her Kimoyo card.

Twenty-three minutes until the Challenge—so eighteen before the path through the forest is clear and the armies break through.

Shuri plants her hands on her hips and shakes her head. "I could've sworn I set that *BLASTED* thing to the twenty-four-hour clock," she says.

Zanda cocks her head, momentarily thrown off—and successfully distracted—by the princess's bizarre declaration. Which gives K'Marah just enough time to react to the code word and toss Shuri the kitty cannon blaster prototype—a cat-shaped, handheld device that shoots bursts of electromagnetic energy from its open maw.

"K'Marah, kill the light!" Shuri fires off two shots—one at Zanda and one at Henbane—and because Zanda's sun shield is hanging at her side, she takes the hit right to the chest and cries out just as the field goes dark.

Henbane manages to dodge, the shot glancing off his right shoulder, but as Shuri takes off running in the direction of the remaining herbs, she hears a grunt and his voice shout, "Ow, not cool!" just before K'Marah says, "You sent me a *poisoned* bracelet? Really?"

Shuri manages a smile as she races toward the remaining plants . . . though what she plans to do when she gets to them, she doesn't know. There are seven herbs left, and as she runs, the number fades to six. Then the sixth one begins to fade. How is she supposed to *stop* something so clearly unstoppable?

So focused on the *what next?* is Shuri, she doesn't notice the figure who steps into her path until a beat too late. She runs smack into Zanda's sun shield and is subsequently blown back as the energy transferred to the shield in the collision is shoved back out into her chest.

All the air is knocked from her lungs when she hits the ground and her CatEyez tumble off. "Oof!" The back of her skull throbs—though she's sure the cushion of her giant bun of braids prevented an actual concussion—and spots appear in her line of vision.

By the time her head clears, there's someone standing over her.

"So young and overconfident," Zanda says, leaning down so Shuri has a better view of her face in the darkness. "Seems to run in the blood."

"Where"—Shuri coughs—"did you get that shield?"

Now Zanda laughs. "Henbane has been moving about your cherished nation for quite some time, Shuri. Poisoning your precious plants and shutting down a swath of the forest were aspects of his assignment, yes. But he learned a few other useful things as well."

"Henbane forged that shield?" As Shuri knows from her own work, crafting an object of that sort is no easy feat.

Pity. *Those* abilities would've been quite useful in a laboratory technician.

Shuri's head drops to the left, and that's when she sees it: one last heart-shaped herb plant still glowing bright. She stares, breath held as her heart sinks into the ground beneath her, awaiting the telltale fade of life.

Waiting . . .

But it doesn't come. The single stalk stays erect, a beacon of light in the darkness, both literal and figurative.

Zanda turns then, and Shuri gasps, cursing herself for her carelessness. "K'Marah—!"

"Henbane!"

They shout the names almost simultaneously, but K'Marah leaps into action first, her Kimoyo light re-illuminated and rigorous Dora Milaje training coming to the fore. Henbane, though, is right on her heels.

But then Zanda is up and headed toward the plant as well.

Shuri scrambles into action, sitting upright and feeling around on the darkened ground for her spectacles. She finds the little cannon blaster first. Knowing there's no time, as soon as her hand closes around it, she takes aim and fires, praying to Bast the shot doesn't hit K'Marah.

It goes wide, but the light from the blast glints off something shiny.

The glasses.

Shuri forces them onto her face and watches in horror as Henbane leaps toward her friend. "K'Marah!"

Shuri is on her feet and dragging her way forward.

And though Henbane barely grazes K'Marah's back with his fingertips, the Dora girl stumbles and collapses in a heap.

"I'm so sorry," Shuri hears him say as he drops to his knees beside her friend and lays a hand on her face. "I didn't have a choice. Zanda was going to kill my grandpapa . . . I left one plant alive—"

"Don't touch her!" Shuri fires another shot, and it hits him square in the left shoulder. He falls back, arm limp and useless at his side.

But it's too late: Zanda has reached the final herb. "Oh, Princess," she says, standing over it, as haughty and triumphant as Shuri's ever seen anyone look. "You try *so* hard. But as you Wakandans will have to learn: Sometimes failure is inevitable."

She reaches down and wraps a hand around the plant's stalk.

"STOP!" Shuri fires a shot at Zanda. Again the woman uses her shield to absorb and redirect the blow. The princess does her best to dodge, but it glances off her leg. "Ahhh!" She collapses as the entire left side of her body goes numb.

"Give UP, Princess!" Zanda shouts, reaching for the herb again.

"NO—"

But her cry is drowned out by an earth-trembling rumble of thunder.

Zanda freezes and looks skyward.

"Oh, you're in *big* trouble now," Shuri says, relief flooding every cell of her body.

Lightning flashes, and illuminated for the briefest of moments is a brown-skinned, white-haired woman, descending from the sky.

20
PRINCESS SHURI

And then the rain begins.

"Ororo!" Zanda shouts, releasing the herb and standing upright in evident panic. "What are *you* doing here?"

"Assisting my family," Storm says, white eyes blazing. "Shuri, you and K'Marah must get down to the baobab plain. The invading armies have broken through—"

"But T'Challa said we were prepared!" Shuri exclaims.

Zanda laughs, briefly distracted from her fear of the Mistress of the Elements. "Arrogant and witless, that T'Challa. Too full of self-importance to recogni—"

"Keep his name out of your wretched mouth!" Storm's eyes flicker, and a rogue gust of wind swirls around Zanda, twisting the thin fabric of her robe, and whipping her long braids into her face.

Shuri chuckles as she watches Zanda's arms flail about, but Ororo's sharp-edged voice brings her back to reality. "Your defenses were able to rout the ranks that made their way through the forest, Princess. But there were two other entry points, both of which went unguarded."

It clicks for Shuri then. "The forest entry was a diversion!"

"A successful one," Zanda shouts triumphantly from the midst of her personal tornado.

"Shut it!" Ororo flicks a hand in Zanda's direction, and the winds around her pick up speed.

"Gah!" Zanda shouts.

"Shuri, you and K'Marah must get down to the baobab plain to warn T'Challa. Two other factions have entered: one through the border with Azania, and one with Canaan. It would appear that both gained entry through tunnels."

"Tunnels?" Shuri says. "But how—" She looks over at where K'Marah is unconscious and Henbane is standing over her, very much not completing his task of killing the final herb. He looks up at Shuri. "Tunnels, too?" she says, and he averts his eyes. "K'Marah certainly knows how to pick a winner . . ." Shuri mumbles.

Henbane peeks over his shoulder at the still-struggling Zanda, then turns to Shuri. "I can wake her," he says, reaching for K'Marah.

"I told you not to touch her!" Shuri levels her cannon blaster at him again. "Get. Away."

He raises his working hand. The other arm is still limp and useless at his side.

"I'm sorry!" he says. "I didn't mean for things to go this far—" He shakes his head.

Shuri eyes him with suspicion. "How do I know you won't just hurt her more?"

"I didn't intend to hurt her at all. She's the only real friend I've ever had and . . . all of this was a mistake. I should not have responded to her message knowing of my mission—"

"Appreciate the heart-to-heart you kids are having, but *there is an invasion happening*. If you could wrap it up . . ." Ororo says.

Henbane drops down and runs his fingertips over K'Marah's cheek—and then quickly backs away.

Which is a smart move. Because as soon as she sits up, fully back to herself and looking like she just had the best night of sleep in her life, she's searching for him, eyes wide, rage heaving in her chest. "Where is he?"

“No time,” Shuri says, pulling her friend to her feet and away from Henbane. She’s more than a little nervous about what she plans to say to the boy, but there aren’t any alternatives. So she steps right into his face. “If you’re *really* sorry, and you care about her, protect that plant with your life.”

“Huh?” K’Marah says. “If he—”

“We gotta move, K’Marah. Wakanda is under attack. We need to get to T’Challa.”

As the *Predator* soars toward the site of the Challenge—which should be getting under way right about now—the girls pass over one of the other two entry points Ororo mentioned. The invading soldiers are flooding out of a hole in the ground at the edge of a patch of forest like deadly siafu ants fleeing a poked mound. Unable to just zip by as though nothing is happening, the princess pulls an astonishing midair U-turn and gets to firing round after round of bright-blue electromagnetic energy bursts into the ranks of interlopers. Depending on where they’re hit, some are blown back, or trip and go sprawling, or are pulled to the ground when the arm holding their weapon goes limp, and gravity takes over.

“YES! Shuri! Knock them dead!” K’Marah shouts with a clap of her hands.

Of the soldiers who manage to evade Shuri's onslaught, only a handful refuse to abort their mission and attempt to press forward toward the baobab field. Most, however, scramble back to their entry point.

"Hold us steady," Shuri says, and K'Marah slides over to take the two-pronged steering mechanism. Then Shuri kneels down. "Full disclosure: I haven't actually tested this particular armament. It is very powerful and lined with Vibranium, and it utilizes kinetic energy collected in flight from contrary winds." There's a *chi-chock* sound as she loads the thing. "I call it the Imperial Blaster."

"Uhh . . ." is all K'Marah can muster.

"There will likely be a recoil."

She fires.

FWOOMP . . . BOOOOOOM!

"Ahhh!" K'Marah screams and bounces into the air as the *Predator* jolts like someone smacked it on the rear.

"Sorry!" Shuri says, taking over the reins again. "Did the trick, though!"

And she's right: There may still be a tunnel beneath the forest floor, but it officially leads to a dead end—the blast remolded the earth and sealed off the exit.

"Onward!" Shuri says. "The guards near the Challenge grounds can handle the stragglers."

It takes three minutes for the girls to reach the edge of the baobab field. "Can you believe just two days ago we were looking down at a gathering of Wakanda's greatest warriors from that ridge over there?" K'Marah says, pointing. "And trying not to be seen?"

"Definitely feels like longer," Shuri replies, circling the perimeter of the field to prepare for landing.

Ororo revealed that she'd considered going to T'Challa herself, but with the Challenge looming, she felt that, as an outsider, interrupting the ritual would give the people of Wakanda the wrong impression. (Politics: barf.)

And though Shuri is a member of the royal family, something about Ororo's reasoning rings in her ears. The elders—Mother included—already feel the princess is frivolous. Adorable at times (she hates when they use that word, *adorable*, like she's one of the border clan's rhinoceros calves), but a nuisance at others.

She has a hunch that if she and K'Marah storm the plain, they'll be leaning into the latter, even if it *is* to shout that enemy forces have invaded.

Shuri parks the *Predator* not too far from the spot where they last laid eyes on T'Challa, and as they exit the vessel, they can hear the rhythmic rumble of drumbeats that precedes the tribal-clan roll call. They creep to where the land begins to slope gently downward, and then drop to a knee to avoid being totally conspicuous—two stalks, one long and reedy, the other short and stocky, but both stark against the horizon were one to look up in their direction.

"So what do we do now?" K'Marah whispers. The procession, where each clan of tribal representatives makes a grand entrance by heavily ornamented caravan, and then takes up their positions around the perimeter of the Challenge Ring—a glorified circle drawn on a patch of land where the grass doesn't grow—is ending as the final two delegations file into position to the beat of the drums. T'Challa has yet to make his grand appearance, but the girls can see the tent he will exit a few meters back from the edge of the ring.

"Oh look, there's Grandmother!" K'Marah says with a point and a smile.

Eldress Umbusi's shoulders and arms are bare, and the gold-and-bronze-threaded halter-tunic she's wearing makes her skin glow that much more. She looks . . . *radiant*. In fact, all the elders have come out in their finest, and from up here on the hill, the clumped clans look like precious gemstones, gathered in piles and glittering in the midafternoon sunlight—rubies, sapphires, emeralds, citrines, amethysts.

"We need to figure out—"

"Hey, S.H.U.R.I.," K'Marah says, "scan the perimeter."

"Scanning the perimeter," comes the reply.

"Hey, she's not supposed to respond to *you*," Shuri protests.

"Shhh."

There's a *ding*.

Shuri continues to scowl into the distance.

"Will you stop being ridiculous and check your Kimoyo card?"

"What for? We're supposed to be forming a plan—"

"So we can see where the final faction of invaders is coming from, duh!" K'Marah shakes her head. "You could never be a Dora Milaje."

"Oh, whatever." Shuri taps the screen of her Kimoyo card so that a hologram of their surroundings within a fifty-kilometer radius floats before their eyes. "There!" she exclaims, pointing out a gap in the woods to the northeast—and the insect-looking figures filing out of it. "That's about a half kilometer away—"

There's a loud and final *BOOM* from the drums, and then the whole plain goes silent. The girls watch the proceedings beneath them, now unable to pull their eyes away.

Okoye and Nakia, who are standing guard to either side of the tent's opening, turn to face each other with a snap.

Then T'Challa steps out.

"Great BAST!" Shuri's hands fly to her mouth, and she turns to K'Marah. "He's wearing the new *habit*! Your uncle must've completed and delivered it!"

Shuri watches spellbound as her unmasked brother, king, and protector of her and her people strides toward the circle. Okoye and Nakia fall into parallel rank a step behind him, staffs in opposite hands, chins slightly aloft. The silence—and reverence—are so absolute, it seems even the creatures of the air have ceased their movement.

A man approaches the opposite end of the Challenge Ring and bows. "My king," he says, loud enough for all to hear. "Thank you for your participation in this, our most sacred of traditions."

Uncle S'Yan.

His pride in his nephew resounds in his deeply resonant voice as he announces the rules of Challenge Day, and sets the ritual in motion.

As he paces around the outer rim of the Sacred Circle, addressing each tribe, drawing a smile here, a laugh there, a shallow bow or expression of sorrow over there . . .

"We have to take care of it," Shuri says, surprising even herself with the words.

"Huh?"

"The intruders." Shuri turns to K'Marah. "They timed this invasion to disrupt one of our oldest and most revered traditions. Distracted us with that forest move, thinking they'd hit us when our king's focus has shifted elsewhere, catch us off guard and use it to their advantage." Zanda's face flashes against the inside of Shuri's eyelids, but not the one from her vision—the one she's seen. That of a haughty—though clearly *delusional*—ruler who would attack a neighboring nation in a grab for power.

Shuri knows one thing: That's not the type of *princess* she ever intends to be.

"But they were wrong," she continues. "Our guard is *not* down, and we will not tolerate such blatant disrespect of our traditions. Which . . . make sense to me now. Even though before they sort of didn't."

K'Marah snorts. "So what's the plan, Your Majesty?"

Down below, Uncle S'Yan shouts, "Do we have a challenger? One who can prove themselves worthy by exhibiting readiness to lay his—or her—life on the line for the safety and welfare of Wakanda?"

Shuri smiles.

T'Challa pulls his mask on and steps into the circle.

"Let's go," Shuri says, not waiting to see if some brave warrior steps forward to face the Black Panther. "Can you pull up that terrain view again so we can send it to the *Predator*'s GPS? No need to send a king when a princess will do."

21
WAKANDA FOREVER

The plan forms as Shuri and K'Marah race back to the *Predator* and climb aboard.

And it's not foolproof. Especially considering how much of it will rely on prototype tech that hasn't been tested on the scale they're about to need it.

But as Shuri and her very best friend rise into the air inside a craft *she* built—a craft that has *safely* taken them from Wakanda to Kenya to London and back over the course of mere days—and she peeks down at the plain where her brother is flipping and kicking and dipping and dodging in the stretchiest suit a Black

Panther has ever known, a sense of purpose as thick and sweet as fresh mango juice slides down her throat and settles in her belly.

She's a princess, yes, but she was *made* to serve and protect her people.

"So where to first?" K'Marah says, taking over the role of navigator without being asked. She taps the map on the central screen, and a bird's-eye view of their immediate surroundings fills the cabin around them. Shuri uses her fingertips to rotate the landscape and zoom in on the target area. The interloping troops have formed ranks nine wide and seven deep . . . so far. There are still little insect-like specks filing out of a barely visible dark spot in a grove of trees.

With a clap, the map zooms out wide, and Shuri is able to see three things: (1) the triumphant group of Wakandan warriors returning from the hole in the forest after routing that particular group of invaders, (2) the captured men who managed to avoid being trapped in the second tunnel by Shuri's Imperial Blaster shot, and (3) a small faction of Wakandan warriors headed to face off against the group coming out of the third hole. As she and K'Marah watch, three figures in rhinoceros hats break off from the Wakandan ranks and run in the direction of the baobab field. Presumably to alert the king.

"Hey, S.H.U.R.I., how far to *this* spot?" Shuri pokes an area on the 3-D map, and it illuminates.

"Approximately twelve-point-eight kilometers, or three minutes and two seconds at the current rate of travel," the robot voice says.

Shuri rubs her chin. "And to the lab?"

"Twenty-three seconds southeast."

"So even with a stop, we could be there in five minutes," Shuri says to no one in particular.

K'Marah presses all ten fingertips together and then pulls them apart to zoom in on the skirmish at the border. The small contingent of Wakandans has reached the fray and is attempting to hold back the advancing army, but it's clear the rhino-hatted border guards could use some backup. If the princess had to guess, there's a good chance the best and brightest warriors were all sent to fight at the dying forest. Which would mean *these* were the guys . . . who were left. "You sure a pit stop is wise?"

Shuri turns the vessel away from the action. "Even if they trounce all of our guys and sprint full speed to the city, it would take a minimum of eleven minutes for the fastest person in the world to run that distance," Shuri says. "Zanda might've got them in—with advanced weaponry, from the looks of it . . ." Three tiny shoots of white light fly through the air from some miniature cannon thing and knock one of the border rhinos over on its side. Its legs continue to kick at the air. "But there are a couple of things she failed to consider."

"Yeah? Like what?"

"Well, *optimal mobility*, for one," Shuri says, gesturing with her chin at the enthusiastic, but discombobulated—and quickly tiring—invading soldiers as she lowers the *Predator* into the opening doors of her laboratory's hangar entrance.

"Noted," K'Marah replies with a nod. "And for two?"

When K'Marah looks over, Shuri is smiling. The princess presses a series of buttons and turns a few dials on the control panel before the rear hatch lowers. She rotates toward it and bounces on her toes.

"For two, she forgot to consider *me*," she says with a wink. "I'll be right back." And she disappears down the ramp and out of sight.

Shuri is back on the Predator, with an odd-looking half sphere in hand, quicker than K'Marah can blink, and within three and a half minutes, they're approaching what has literally become a battlefield. "Wow, that sure took a turn," K'Marah says as they get closer.

And she's not wrong: The number of interlopers

has . . . multiplied. To a point that seems, if not impossible, *highly* implausible.

"Where on earth did they all come from?" Shuri says to no one in particular.

"Well, looking at the map, I'd guess Niganda and Canaan," K'Marah says, bringing her palms together over the 3-D landscape to zoom out. "They're coming in beneath the part of the forest that borders on both countries. Is there a way to see the tunnel on this thing?"

Shuri nods and taps a screen to her left. The projected landscape turns white, and a long, thick red line appears at the southwest edge. "Infrared mode," she says. "It utilizes thermal readings and isolates—"

"Save it, Sherlock. We gotta stop this NOW. There are more of them coming." As K'Marah hyperzooms on the tunnel, Shuri sees exactly what she means: The thing is *full* of weapon-carrying men, three flush in a line that extends a quarter of the distance to the border—which is over a kilometer and a half away.

Shuri gulps. She's tempted to ask her AI for a count of the intruders—there have to be over a thousand—but decides against it. Maybe better not to know *exactly* what they're up against.

"We do have a plan . . ." K'Marah looks up, panic splashed over her face like a hastily thrown cup of ice water. "Right?"

Shuri continues to stare at the holographic rendering of a piece of her homeland she's never even seen up close. How many other corners of Wakanda has she yet to explore? How many treasures has she yet to find?

What will happen if she fails at *this* mission?

"Shuri?" K'Marah's dread is palpable now.

Shuri *cannot* fail. She *must* not.

She can *do* this. She can beat them.

She can.

She just hopes all the Wakandans who answered the call to defense did so because they were wearing their communication bracelets.

"Hey, S.H.U.R.I., highlight all the Kimoyo beads within this region." Shuri circles the area on the map where most of the moving bodies are gathered. A few stragglers have made their way farther in, but for the most part, the Nigandans/Narobians/Canaanites/*whoever* haven't made a ton of progress in their march on the city.

"Highlighting Kimoyo beads," the AI says.

About a hundred of the mini people on the map turn purple . . . and not all of them are in motion.

K'Marah gasps. "Are those ones—"

"Let's not think about it right now," Shuri says, stepping up to the *Predator*'s control panel. She manually shifts into hover mode, and the aircraft slows to a stop with the thick of the melee still a couple of hundred meters or so in front of them. Then she slides to the left and pushes a button. A hidden screen flips into view, and she taps a series of numbers into it before a lever slides out of a concealed slot in the ceiling.

"Sheesh, how many secret doodads does this thing have?"

Shuri grins at her friend, confidence renewed. "If only you knew," she says. "Hey, S.H.U.R.I., activate Kimoyo Capture."

"Kimoyo Capture activated." All the purple people turn green.

She cautiously wraps a hand around the lever then. And takes a deep breath. "You, uhh, might want to buckle up," she says to K'Marah.

"Why?" (Though the shorter girl scrambles into the co-captain's chair and fastens herself in before Shuri has a chance to answer.)

"There might be a small jolt. Though it'll be way worse for *them* . . ."

"WAI—"

Shuri shoves the lever forward—

And is almost thrown back as every human body below with a Kimoyo bead attached to it is wrapped in a tiny force field and pulled three or so meters into the air, out of the reach of enemy hands.

"By *BAST*!" K'Marah gasps. She turns to Shuri, thunderstruck. "I guess that *does* come in handy! How does it work again?"

Shuri reaches forward with her free hand and turns a dial. The bodies begin to move toward them *very* quickly—"Whoops! Too fast!" she says—then slower as she reverses the dial the slightest bit. She and K'Marah can both see some of the person-filled bubbles shifting shape as the inhabitants squirm and flail within them. "It's a simple mechanism, really," she begins. "I use the Kimoyo tech to create an electromagnetic field around each individual utilizing their body heat—"

"Nope, never mind." K'Marah lifts a hand. "What next?"

"Well, uhhh . . ." Shuri focuses in on a section of the map projection . . . but doesn't let go of the lever or the dial. She glares at it for a moment, narrowing her eyes.

"Umm, Shuri? Hello? Next?"

The princess's forehead wrinkles as her concentration intensifies.

And then her face goes slack and she drops her chin. "Can you take your finger and circle that open area on the other side of the stream we just crossed? South of the baobab plain."

K'Marah doesn't respond, and when Shuri looks

up, she sees that her dear friend is smirking. "You can't let go of those things, huh, genius?"

"I truly despise you sometimes."

K'Marah does as Shuri requested, snickering the whole time, and as soon as all the floating Wakandan soldiers have entered the target area—as indicated by a **ding* and the space turning yellow on the floating map—Shuri cranks the dial to zero, carefully lets go, and then slowly pulls the lever back to lower the soldiers back down.

The force fields vanish, and both girls watch, relieved, as most of the little figures plop to the ground, then stagger to their feet, confused but safe.

"Whew!" Shuri says, lifting her hand for K'Marah to high-five. "Phase one complete." She spreads her arms wide and brings her hands together in a clap. The map folds and vanishes, returning the cabin to its *regular* overly high-tech state, then Shuri turns back to the control panel, shifts out of hover mode, and eases them into motion in the direction of the invaders.

"Let me guess: Phase one was the easy part," K'Marah says, coming to stand at Shuri's side.

"Mmmm . . . You could say that."

"Figures."

The girls lapse into silence as the horde of invaders comes into full view before them.

"There are so *many*," K'Marah continues, breathless.

Shuri doesn't respond to that. She just begins a slow descent over the re-forming ranks, shifting into hover when they're right over the center.

"We're invisible right now, yes?" K'Marah asks.

"Yes," Shuri says with a confident nod.

But then she looks down.

It would seem the invaders have been reenergized by the whisking away of Wakanda's warriors. As they re-form their ranks and march onward, they hit their shields against their chests and chant some kind of battle cry.

It shakes the princess. "K'Marah?"

"Whatever you're planning, it's going to work." The soon-to-be Dora turns to Shuri and puts a hand on her friend's shoulder. "Okay?"

Shuri's heart rate increases, and she faces back forward. Her eyes sweep the masses below again, and she opens her mouth to speak, but all that comes out is a strange squawk she had no idea her throat could make.

"Maybe it'll help if you . . ." K'Marah takes an audible centering breath. ". . . explain the science of your plan. To me."

And then the world opens and a light turns on. "Really?" Shuri says.

"Mm-hmm!" K'Marah forces a smile.

Which is more than enough for the princess. Setting her nerves on a back burner, she kicks into high gear. "Okay, so I've been secretly working on some new security tech." She squats and pulls a rounded, though flat-bottomed, black object etched with glowing purple lines from a compartment beneath the control panel. "This hemisphere," she says, holding it up, "is what I returned to the lab to retrieve. I call it the Dome. It's merely a prototype, but my hope is that through the use of a spectrometer, I will be able to mimic its shape and create an impenetrable force field around a predetermined area."

She tucks the half sphere under one arm and, with brows pinched and tongue poking out, begins to tap, pinch, shift, and slide her fingers around the main navigation screen. When there's a perfect circle encompassing the tunnel exit *and* all the foreign soldiers—which is easier than she expected it to be considering their insistence on moving in ranks—she nods with satisfaction. Then she drops down again, lifts a hatch in the floor, and lowers the glowy purple-black thingy into it.

She closes the compartment, and stands. Returns to her controls. "If this works like I hope it will, the spectrometer will create the parameters, and the Vibranium released from the Dome will follow the photonic pathway and bind with the carbon molecules along it.

Creating . . . a dome. The intruders will be trapped inside."

"Oh! Like a high-tech snow globe!" K'Marah looks ready to burst, she's so excited to understand.

"Precisely!" Shuri says.

"And then what?"

"And then T'Chal—I mean, the king . . ." Shuri steels herself. They've been so busy, she has no idea if he won the Challenge. "The king can decide what to do with them."

K'Marah nods. "Excellent plan." Then she turns to the princess. "So you ready?"

Shuri presses a button beneath the center of the control panel, and two little doors slide open as another hidden lever rises up. She grabs hold of it. "I was born ready."

"YOU TOTALLY WATCH AMERICAN MOVIES, TOO!" K'Marah shouts.

Shuri smirks.

And shoves the lever forward.

Neither girl speaks as the Dome descends, but Shuri *knows* it is by far the coolest thing she's ever created. They watch as what looks like a flickering liquid pours down over an invisible, upside-down bowl. Even the invading troops look up in awe.

There's a *ding* before the S.H.U.R.I.'s voice rings

out. "Dome deployment complete," it says.

Shuri and K'Marah look at each other.

"Is that . . . it?" the Dora says.

"Guess there's only one way to find out."

Shuri sets the *Predator* down a reasonable distance away: close enough to investigate and get back to the vessel quickly if need be, but far enough away to give them a head start if they have to flee.

Then they get out.

"Here goes," Shuri says, prepping her Kimoyo bracelet to fire temporary-paralysis pulses from the inside of the wrist, spider guy style just in case.

"Shuri . . . look," K'Marah says, pointing. She turns to the princess with a smile.

And Shuri can't help but smile back. Because it's clear from the men banging on the inside of the invisible structure, creating little outward ripples of light (perhaps she should electrify the thing?), that they're trapped inside.

It worked.

"You did it!" K'Marah says, leaping onto her friend.

Shuri barely catches the shorter girl. "*WE* did it." The girls hug. "You and me. Together—"

"Guess that means you should be punished together, eh?" comes a familiar voice from behind them.

Shuri shuts her eyes.

"Oh boy," K'Marah says.

"Lies upon lies upon lies. I don't know what's gotten into you, Shuri, and I am much too civilized to try to paddle it out. But know that you have quite a bit of explaining to do—"

"You too, K'Marah!" comes a second adult female voice.

"Ugh," K'Marah sighs. "Guess I'm in trouble, too."

"Likely," Shuri says.

And then she takes a deep breath. "Turn around and face the music on three?"

"Let's just get it over with . . ."

So both girls turn. And as they look into the furious faces of the queen mother and Eldress Umbusi, they know: The battle might have been won, but the war has yet to begin.

MISSION LOG

I AM "GROUNDED." (CLEARLY EVEN MOTHER CAN'T RESIST AMERICAN TELEVISION SHOWS ON PANTHERTUBE.)

Indefinitely, was the answer I received when I asked, "For how long?" but considering the success of my Dome technology and the fact that our Ministry of Defense is now clamoring to figure out how to expand it—the mechanized forest has been deemed "insufficient security" after the events of Challenge Day—I'm certain this bizarre punishment won't last for long.

While K'Marah and I were trying to save the nation, three brave souls stepped forward to challenge T'Challa. And in his new kinetic-energy absorbing, hyperstretchy Panther Habit, he trounced them all.

Was our *king* stunned to regain access to his technology and immediately learn that over the course of the seventeen-minute Challenge, a full-on ground invasion *had* taken place? Yes.

But he was also grateful. For me. His darling "zeal"-filled baby sister who clearly has more "wisdom and foresight" than he possesses in his little finger. SO grateful was he, in fact, he convinced Mother of my need for tactical, weapons, and combat training.

In regard to the foreign troops: The sixteen or so that managed to progress ahead of the others were all caught and arrested. The ones *within* the Dome were so shaken by first seeing the Wakandan warriors literally lifted from the fray, carried away in midair, and then finding themselves entrapped within a structure that came down around them like a lowering glass goblet, none of them moved when the Dome vanished, and Wakanda's finest warriors—led by the Dora Milaje, of course—surrounded them on all sides. T'Challa said many of them bowed to him as he approached, convinced he was a god. (Like his head needs to be any bigger.)

After confiscating their weapons and having their hands bound, T'Challa had them escorted back to the tunnel in groups of thirty and let them leave the way they had come.

I'm sure—as he is—that they won't return.

And thanks to Ororo, Zanda was placed in a capsule with her very own tornado swirling around her, and hand-delivered to the Narobian capital. She'll be fine provided they figure out how to extract her without unleashing the live cyclone on the city.

Henbane has been detained and is awaiting trial. There was, of course, more to his story than Zanda let on: While he *was* discovered in the act of killing some rude rich man's mango trees, he only took the "job" with Zanda because she claimed she could connect him with members of the family he's never known.

When she purported to have discovered a grandfather of his, he latched on like a drowning man to a life preserver, so desperate was he for family. He did everything she asked of him, despite the fact that she continued to pile on demands that had to be met before she'd "reunite" them.

He got suspicious, of course. But then she began to threaten first Henbane, then this grandpapa, with death if Henny didn't do precisely as she directed. And at that point, what could he have done? Even if there was no grandpapa (and unfortunately, there wasn't), he was in too deep. Zanda was the *ruler* of Narobia, and Henbane is only fourteen.

But the interesting twist: that final herb? He deliberately left it alive. It remained when we returned to the Sacred Field.

Which brings me to the real reason for this log: Through a bit of trial and error over the past few days, I just figured out a way to rid the heart-shaped herb cells of Henbane's toxin—which, it turns out, is a mutated version of the poison found in the plant from which "Henbane" derived his name (his given name is Larry, apparently).

Long story short, by immersing the desiccated roots in a hypertonic solution made of water and the fishy-smelling goop I extracted from previous plants (of all things!), I'm able to stimulate osmosis and force the toxin out. Then after a time in a *hypo*tonic solution of water that has been purified through *reverse* osmosis and infused with Vibranium, the cells fix themselves.

It will take a while to regrow a solid crop, but that's okay.

For now, our nation's (pssst . . . *my*) future is safe.

Wakanda forever.

THE END.

Photo by Rachel Moron

NIC STONE is the *New York Times* bestselling author of the novels *Dear Martin* and *Odd One Out*. She was born and raised in a suburb of Atlanta, Georgia, and the only thing she loves more than an adventure is a good story about one. After graduating from Spelman College, she worked extensively in teen mentoring and lived in Israel for a few years before returning to the United States to write full-time. Having grown up with a wide range of cultures, religions, and back-grounds, she strives to bring diverse voices and stories into her work. Learn more at nicstone.info.

COLLECT THEM ALL!

Set of 4 Hardcover Books ISBN: 978-1-5321-4772-2

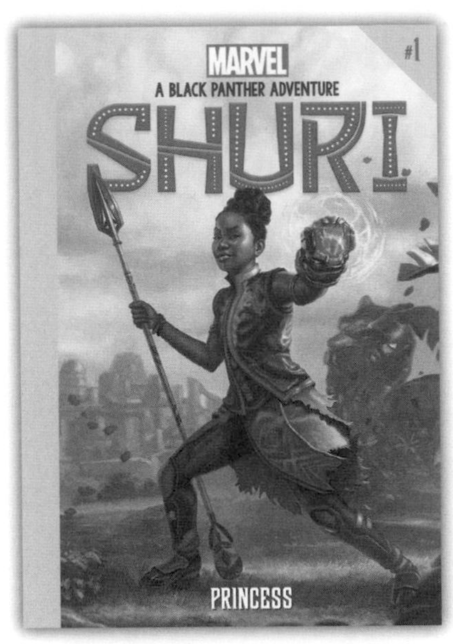

Hardcover Book ISBN
978-1-5321-4773-9

Hardcover Book ISBN
978-1-5321-4774-6

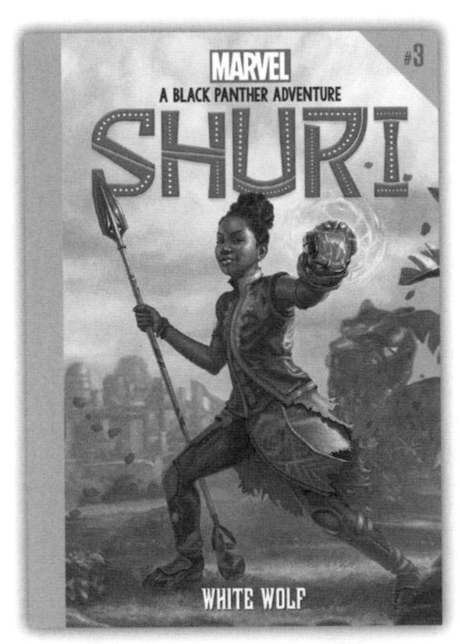

Hardcover Book ISBN
978-1-5321-4775-3

Hardcover Book ISBN
978-1-5321-4776-0